A, B, C, D, Tummy, Toes, Hands, Knees

A, B, C, D,
Tummy, Toes, Hands,
Knees

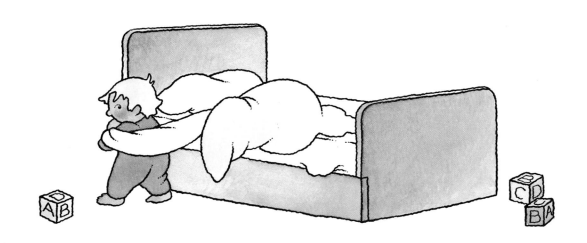

By B. G. HENNESSY · Pictures by WENDY WATSON

VIKING KESTREL

VIKING KESTREL
Published by the Penguin Group
Viking Penguin Inc., 40 West 23rd Street, New York, New York 10010, U.S.A.
Penguin Books Ltd, 27 Wrights Lane, London W8 5TZ, England
Penguin Books Australia Ltd, Ringwood, Victoria, Australia
Penguin Books Canada Ltd, 2801 John Street, Markham, Ontario, Canada L3R 1B4
Penguin Books (N.Z.) Ltd, 182–190 Wairau Road, Auckland 10, New Zealand
Penguin Books Ltd, Registered Offices: Harmondsworth, Middlesex, England

First published in 1989 by Viking Penguin Inc.
Published simultaneously in Canada

1 3 5 7 9 10 8 6 4 2
Text copyright © B.G. Hennessy, 1989
Illustrations copyright © Wendy Watson, 1989
All rights reserved

Library of Congress Cataloging-in-Publication Data
Hennessy, B. G. (Barbara G.) A,B,C,D, tummy, toes, hands, knees
by B.G. Hennessy; illustrated by Wendy Watson.   p.   cm.
Summary: Listed rhyming words and simple illustrations depict how a mother
and baby spend the day together delighting in the world and each other.
ISBN 0-670-81703-1   [1. Babies—Fiction. 2. Mother and child—Fiction.
3. Stories in rhyme.]   I. Watson, Wendy, ill.   II. Title.
III. Title: ABCD, tummy, toes, hands, knees.
PZ8.3.H418Aam   1989   [E]—dc19   88-32225

Color Separations by Imago Ltd., Hong Kong
Manufactured by Imago Ltd., Hong Kong
Set in Bembo.

For Mark Andrew

Bowl, Spoon, Plate, Cup

Kitten, Bunny, Little Pup

A, B, C, D

Tummy, Toes, Hands, Knees

Shirt, Socks, Shoes, Hat

Duck, Cow, Horse, Cat

Apple, Banana, Peach, Pear

Blanket, Stroller, Teddy Bear

Tree, Bird, Bush, Flower

Bridge, Tunnel, Road, Tower

1, 2, 3, 4

Roof, Chimney, Window, Door

Up, Down, In, Between

Red, Yellow, Blue, Green

Walk, Run,

Jump, Fall

Blocks, Cars, Book, Ball

Crash, Boom

Bang, Thud

Pebbles, Rocks

Dirt, Mud

Bath, Towel, Soap, Bubbles

Splash, Kick,

Little Puddles

Lap,
Clap,

Peek-a-Boo

Kisses, Hugs

I Love You.

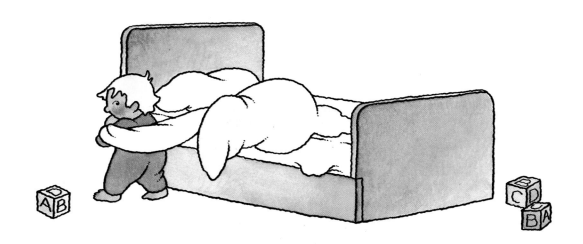